Detective mazes

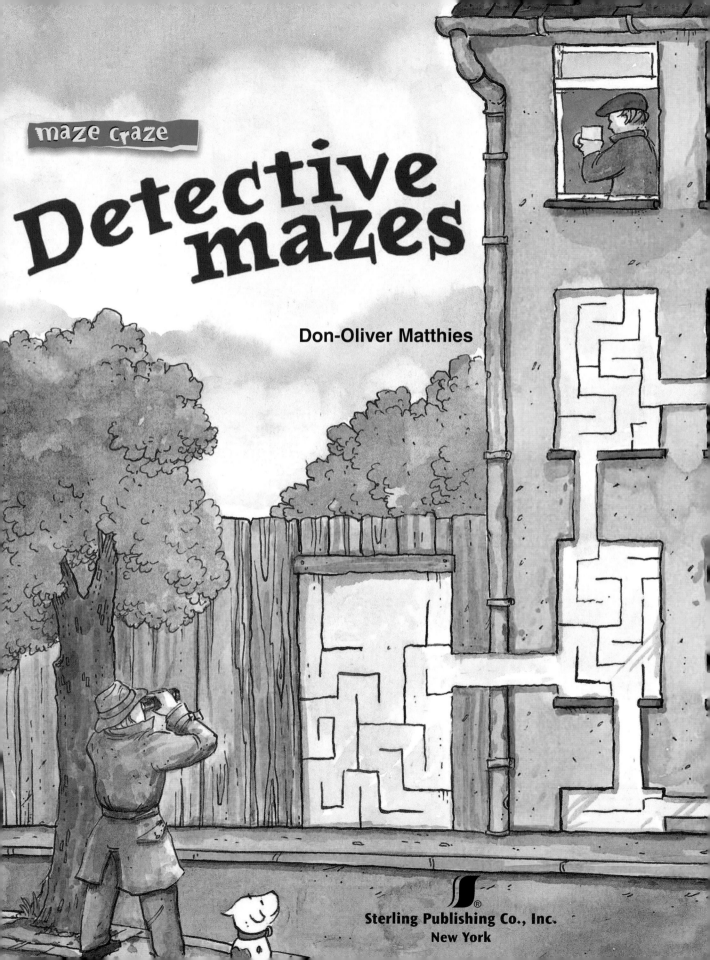

maze craze

Detective mazes

Don-Oliver Matthies

Sterling Publishing Co., Inc.
New York

Library of Congress Cataloging-in-Publication Data Available

20 19 18 17 16 15 14 13 12   0 5 / 2 0 1 2

Published in 2004 by Sterling Publishing Co., Inc.
387 Park Avenue South
New York, NY 10016
Originally published in Germany in 2003 under the title
Detektiv auf heißer Spur by Edition Bücherbär im Arena
Verlag GmbH, Rottendorfer Str. 16, D-97074 Würzburg
Copyright © 2003 by Edition Bücherbär im Arena Verlag GmbH
English translation © 2004 by Sterling Publishing Co., Inc.
Distributed in Canada by Sterling Publishing
^C/o Canadian Manda Group, 165 Dufferin Street
Toronto, Ontario, Canada, M6K 3H6
Distributed in the United Kingdom by GMC Distribution Services,
Castle Place, 166 High Street, Lewes, East Sussex, England BN7 1XU
Distributed in Australia by Capricorn Link (Australia) Pty Ltd.
P.O. Box 704, Windsor, NSW 2756, Australia

Printed in China

Sterling ISBN-13: 978-1-4027-1293-7
       ISBN-10: 1-4027-1293-6

For information about custom editions, special sales, premium and
corporate purchases, please contact Sterling Special Sales
Department at 800-805-5489 or specialsales@sterlingpub.com

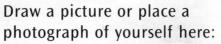
Draw a picture or place a photograph of yourself here:

This book belongs to:

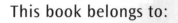

This is Detective Watts, a private investigator, and his bloodhound Sniff. Whenever he's not busy solving tricky cases, he tries his hand at mazes.

In his office, Detective Watts goes over some of his old cases. It's not always easy to connect pieces of evidence with the individual criminals.

The telephone rings. There was a break-in at the museum, and the thieves made off with two prized paintings.

Detective Watts and Sniff immediately hop onto their motorcycle and zip over to the museum.

start

end

8

start

end

The museum's curator is there to meet Detective Watts when he arrives. Quite flustered, he explains which paintings are missing. He wonders how the detective will track down the thieves.

Detective Watts sets out immediately on a search for clues. He can already figure out how the robbers got into the museum.

With his magnifying glass, the detective searches for fingerprints on the shards of glass from the broken window.

Watts discovers footprints in the yard. Can you follow the path that the thieves took from the window to the fence?

13

In front of the fence, Detective Watts finds tire tracks from the thieves' car. Can you match the cars to their tracks?

Back at his office, Detective Watts searches his computer's files for suspects. After many hours of research, he comes up with a likely suspect: Bruno.

end

start

15

Detective Watts knows Bruno well. He's stolen paintings before. It's time for a secret stakeout, so Watts disguises himself in a gray trench coat.

The detective makes his way to Bruno's apartment. Hiding near a tree, Detective Watts watches his every move.

end

start

A blue delivery truck is parked near the apartment. Detective Watts believes the tire tracks he found earlier could belong to this truck.

Detective Watts and Sniff follow the crafty thief through the city.

Bruno drives to an old warehouse. Hidden in the basement, his partners in crime are waiting for him.

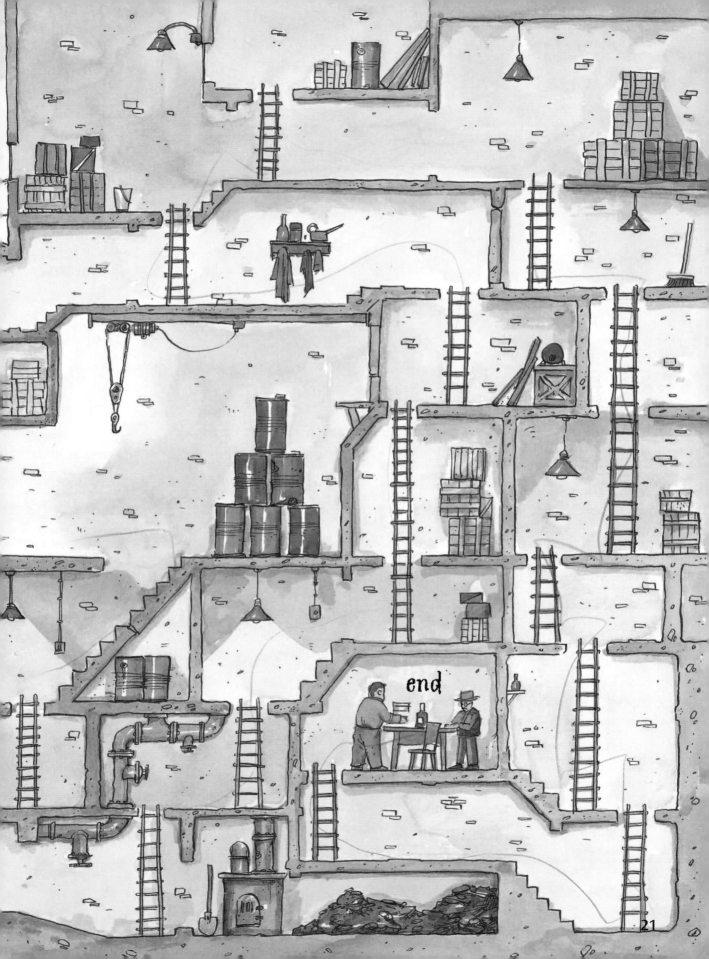

end

Bruno and his fellow criminal friends sit down to celebrate their successful getaway. The Professor, who really isn't a professor, is smart and crafty and therefore plans the crimes. Al isn't as smart as the Professor, but he's twice as strong.

After dinner, the robbers plan their next big burglary. They plan to break into the bank, sneak past the night watchmen, and cut open the safe. Detective Watts overhears everything.

While the thieves are busy scheming, Detective Watts quickly searches the basement. Perhaps the paintings are hidden somewhere here?

Sure enough, the detective finds the paintings in one of the boxes. To his surprise, he finds several other stolen items as well. From which places were these items taken?

Detective Watts immediately calls the police. He gives them the address of the warehouse and urges the officers to hurry.

The police quickly come and surround the warehouse. The officer in charge asks Detective Watts exactly where the thieves are in the warehouse.

The thieves try to escape, but with so many officers chasing them, they don't stand a chance.

The thieves are brought before the court and sentenced to several years in jail.

The three thieves now have years to just sit and think about their crimes in prison. "Stealing is not worth it," thinks Al. "Next time, I will not let myself get caught," thinks Bruno. The Professor, who wants nothing to do with crime ever again, draws mazes on the cell wall.

Detective Watts, Sniff, and the museum curator celebrate the return of the stolen paintings to the museum.

But soon enough, the next phone call comes. Someone has robbed a rich countess of her jewels. How will she get them back? This is surely a case for Detective Watts and Sniff.

Answers

page 6

John = 3
Dave = 2
Tony = 5
Paul = 4
Bert = 1

page 7

page 8

34

page 9

page 10

page 11

pages 12–13

A = 3
B = 2
C = 1

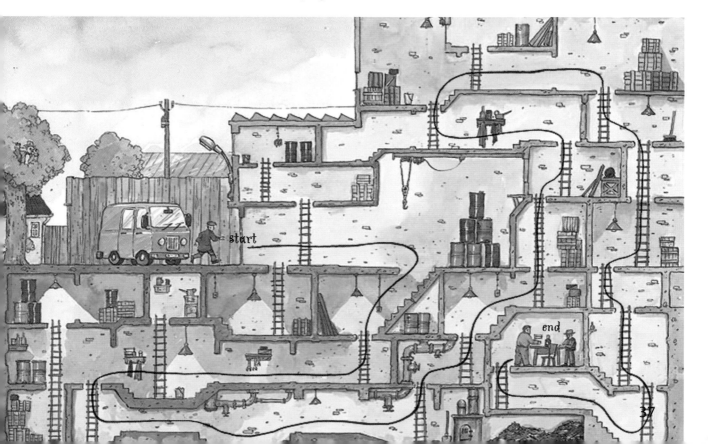

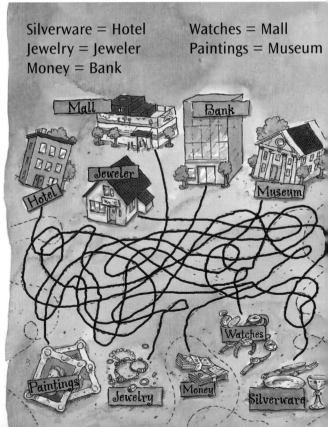

A = 1
B = 4
C = 2
D = 3

page 30

page 31

page 32

page 33

1 = B
2 = D
3 = E
4 = A
5 = C

40